A Note to Parents and Caregivers:

Read-it! Readers are for children who are just starting on the amazing road to reading. These beautiful books support both the acquisition of reading skills and the love of books.

 The PURPLE LEVEL presents basic topics and objects using high frequency words and simple language patterns.

 The RED LEVEL presents familiar topics using common words and repeating sentence patterns.

 The BLUE LEVEL presents new ideas using a larger vocabulary and varied sentence structure.

 The YELLOW LEVEL presents more challenging ideas, a broad vocabulary, and wide variety in sentence structure.

 The GREEN LEVEL presents more complex ideas, an extended vocabulary range, and expanded language structures.

 The ORANGE LEVEL presents a wide range of ideas and concepts using challenging vocabulary and complex language structures.

When sharing a book with your child, read in short stretches, pausing often to talk about the pictures. Have your child turn the pages and point to the pictures and familiar words. And be sure to reread favorite stories or parts of stories.

There is no right or wrong way to share books with children. Find time to read with your child, and pass on the legacy of literacy.

Adria F. Klein, Ph.D.
Professor Emeritus
California State University
San Bernardino, California

Editor: Christianne Jones
Page Production: Tracy Kaehler
Creative Director: Keith Griffin
Editorial Director: Carol Jones

First American edition published in 2006 by
Picture Window Books
5115 Excelsior Boulevard
Suite 232
Minneapolis, MN 55416
877-845-8392
www.picturewindowbooks.com

First published in 2005 by
Allegra Publishing Limited
Unit 13/15 Quayside Lodge
William Morris Way
Townmead Road
London SW6 2UZ UK

Printed in the United States of America.

Library of Congress Cataloging-in-Publication Data
Law, Felicia.
Rumble meets Harry Hippo / by Felicia Law ; illustrated by Yoon-Mi Pak.
p. cm. — (Read-it! readers)
Summary: As Rumble the dragon and Shelby Spider watch, Harry Hippo loads
passengers onto a boat to bring them to Rumble's Cave Hotel. Everything is
fine until Eli Elephant comes aboard and rocks the boat.
ISBN 1-4048-1338-1 (hardcover)
[1. Ferries—Fiction. 2. Elephants—Fiction. 3. Hippopotamus—Fiction.
4. Animals—Fiction.] I. Pak, Yoon Mi, ill. II. Title. III. Series.

PZ7.L41835Rumh 2005
[E]—dc22
                                                    2005027179

Rumble Meets Harry Hippo

by Felicia Law
illustrated by Yoon-Mi Pak

Special thanks to our advisers for their expertise:

Adria F. Klein, Ph.D.
Professor Emeritus, California State University
San Bernardino, California

Susan Kesselring, M.A.
Literacy Educator
Rosemount–Apple Valley–Eagan (Minnesota) School District

PiCTURE WiNDOW BOOKS
Minneapolis, Minnesota

This is the life of a cool, young dragon named Rumble. When his grandma leaves her run-down cave to him, Rumble sets about making it into a four-star hotel. He doesn't do it all alone. He has help from a picky hotel inspector and an annoying spider named Shelby.

Rumble's Cave Hotel has a new
boat to bring guests across the
lake to the hotel. Harry Hippo is
the boat's captain. When Eli
Elephant squeezes on with all of
the other passengers, the boat
starts to wobble. Will Harry Hippo
be able to keep the boat afloat?

Down in the valley, below Rumble's Cave Hotel, stretched a sparkling blue lake. Rumble stood in the doorway and gazed at the pretty water.

He could see the hotel's boat crossing the lake. He could see the passengers on board.

"They're coming!" he called to Shelby Spider. "The passengers are coming!"

7

But the passengers were NOT coming.

They had bought tickets. They had boarded
the boat. They had asked Harry Hippo to
take them across the lake. They had set off
in the right direction, but everything started
to go wrong.

"All aboard!" called Harry Hippo. "Move along! Please take your seats."

Wilson Wolf pushed past Sylvia and Sally Swan. Sylvia and Sally Swan pushed past Keesha Kangaroo. Keesha Kangaroo pushed past Penny Panther. Penny Panther pushed past Wally Warthog. Wally Warthog gave an angry snort, and everyone finally sat down.

11

Then, Eli Elephant came on board. He pushed past Wally Warthog, Penny Panther, Keesha Kangaroo, Sylvia and Sally Swan, and Wilson Wolf. He sat himself down in the front of the boat.

The back of the boat shot straight up, and all of the passengers fell off their seats.

13

14

"This won't work," said Harry Hippo.
"Eli Elephant must sit in the back.
Everyone else must sit in the front."

So, Wilson Wolf pushed past Sylvia and
Sally Swan. Sylvia and Sally Swan pushed
past Keesha Kangaroo. Keesha Kangaroo
pushed past Penny Panther. Penny Panther
pushed past Wally Warthog. Wally
Warthog gave an angry snort, and
everyone finally sat down.

Then, Eli Elephant pushed past Wally
Warthog and Penny Panther and Keesha
Kangaroo and Sylvia and Sally Swan and
Wilson Wolf and sat himself down at the
back of the boat.

But that didn't work, either. The front of the boat shot straight up, and all of the passengers fell off their seats.

"This won't work," said Harry Hippo.
"Eli Elephant must sit in the middle. Half of you must sit in the back. Half of you must sit in the front."

So everyone stood up and Wilson Wolf pushed past ...

Well, you know what happened next.

19

Harry Hippo was pleased.
It looked as if the boat
was finally stable.

"Hold on tight! Please have
your tickets ready," he called.

I penny
round-trip

Then he started up the engine, and
the boat moved across the lake.

Now, if everyone had sat very still and behaved, things might have gone well.

After all, the view was perfect. The lake was calm. The sky was blue. The forest was alive with flowers and birds. It was lovely to see.

But Joe the Joey couldn't see. He was stuffed inside Keesha Kangaroo's pouch. So Joe squeezed and wiggled and wiggled and squeezed—until out he popped.

"POP!" he yelled as he fell over the side of the boat.

23

"Man overboard!" grunted Wally Warthog.

"Get the lifeboats!" bellowed Eli Elephant.

"Women and children first!" squawked Sylvia and Sally Swan.

"Please sit down!" cried Harry Hippo.

But nobody listened.

"Don't worry," said Keesha Kangaroo. "I'll get him." And she dove into the lake with a splash!

Everyone rushed to the side of the boat to watch the excitement. The boat leaned dangerously to one side.

"Let me see," said Eli Elephant, pushing his way through.

27

28

That was too much! Over went the boat!

Plop! went
Wilson Wolf.

Plop! Plop! went
Sylvia and Sally Swan.

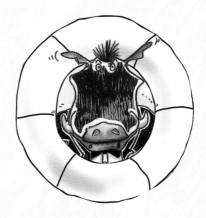

Plop! went
Penny Panther.

Plop! went
Wally Warthog.

SPLASH! went Eli Elephant.

"Oh, dear!" said Rumble, watching the line of dripping guests as they climbed the hill to the hotel. "We'd better get Milly the Maid to bring some warm towels."

The guests were a sorry sight. They stood in the hall, shivering and dripping.

"Ugh!" said Shelby Spider. "Don't come near me! I don't want to get wet!"

"Achoo!" sneezed Eli Elephant as he blew water all over Shelby Spider.

Oh, dear! Poor Shelby! And on that note, all of the wet guests started to laugh.

More *Read-it!* Readers

Bright pictures and fun stories help you practice your reading skills. Look for more books at your level.

Alex and Sarah 1-4048-1352-7

Alex and the Team Jersey 1-4048-1024-2

Alex and Toolie 1-4048-1027-7

Clever Cat 1-4048-0560-5

Felicio's Incredible Invention 1-4048-1030-7

Flora McQuack 1-4048-0561-3

Izzie's Idea 1-4048-0644-X

Joe's Day at Rumble's Cave Hotel 1-4048-1339-X

Naughty Nancy 1-4048-0558-3

Parents Do the Weirdest Things! 1-4048-1031-5

The Princess and the Frog 1-4048-0562-1

The Princess and the Tower 1-4048-1184-2

Rumble Meets Lucas Lizard 1-4048-1334-9

Rumble Meets Randy Rabbit 1-4048-1337-3

Rumble Meets Shelby Spider 1-4048-1286-5

Rumble Meets Todd Toad 1-4048-1340-3

Rumble Meets Vikki Viper 1-4048-1342-X

Rumble the Dragon's Cave 1-4048-1353-5

Rumble's Famous Granny 1-4048-1336-5

The Truth About Hansel and Gretel 1-4048-0559-1

Willie the Whale 1-4048-0557-5

Looking for a specific title or level? A complete list of *Read-it!* Readers is available on our Web site: **www.picturewindowbooks.com**